stop means STOP

Gay Wasik-Zegel

Illustrated by Lorrie J. Smith

D1314729

Cricket Cottage Publishing

ISBN: 1489589414
ISBN-13: 978-1489589415

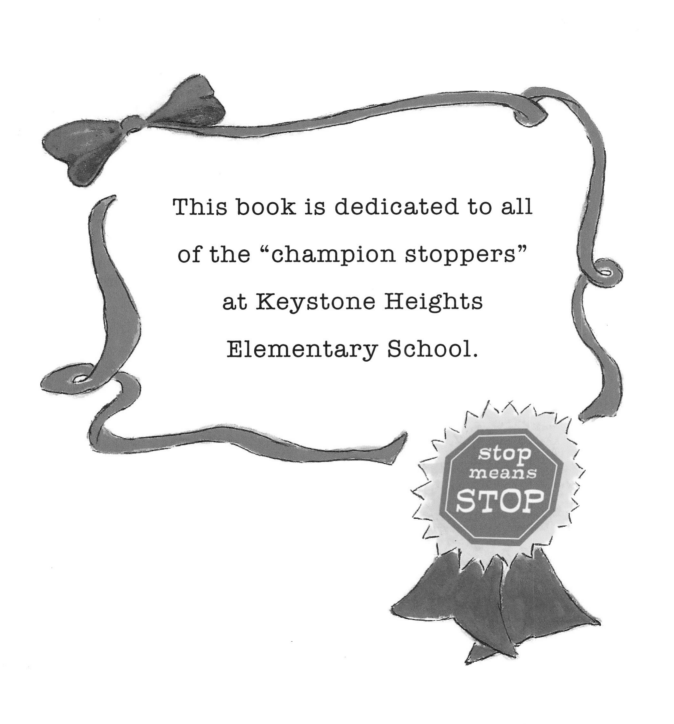

This book is dedicated to all of the "champion stoppers" at Keystone Heights Elementary School.

stop means STOP

From the day he was born,
Charlie rarely was still.
He was robust and healthy
and never got ill.

Tho' his parents were glad
when he learned how to hop,

they wondered,
quite frankly,
if he'd ever **STOP**!

As a toddler he
babbled and wouldn't
stop talking.

At night he would often
do lots of sleepwalking.

He'd run in the house,
or play close to the street.
He'd jump on the sofa.
He'd stand in his seat.

He'd talk out of turn without
waiting to speak,
then go flush the toilet until
it would leak.

When he rode his bicycle
into their pool,
Charlie's parents decided to
enroll him in school.

In class, he was smart and finished up first.
Then he'd laugh and erupt with some silly outburst.
"**Stop** that behavior!" the teacher would say,
but Charlie would laugh and continue to play.

At recess the whistle meant
stop, get a drink.
But he'd keep on going,
which caused quite a stink.

In Music he sang when the song was all through.
His lunch he stuffed in without stopping to chew.

"Stop means stop!"
said the Principal, finding him there.
Charlie nodded then proceeded to
bounce from his chair.

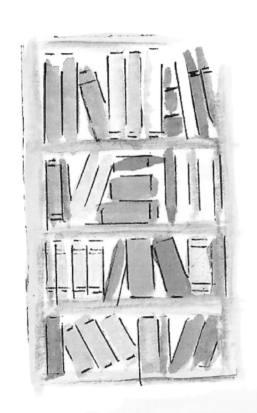

Then one day in Library, things grew quite clear. "**Stop**" was a word he had learned not to hear.

While the others cleaned up and
pushed in their seats,
Charlie paid no attention, just
kept tapping his feet.

"Come with me now!"
said the library teacher.
She showed him a book that's
a reference feature.

"This book gives the meanings
of words that we use.
Find '**stop**' using guide words
on top as your clues."

Charlie froze as he read the word's short definitions. How wrong he had been about his life's ambitions. At once he saw "**stop**" as an active word too. There are moments when "**STOP**" is all you can do.

That night Charlie acted much
like a new child.
He cleaned up his toys and
was not a bit wild.
He turned off his lights, said
his prayers, went to bed.
His parents both feared he had
damaged his head!

The next day when firemen
came into the school
His "**stop, drop,** and **roll**"
practice really looked cool.

In "Computers" he stopped
at just the right spot
to finish each sentence with
a small little dot .

He learned how to "**chill**"
and he learned to act proper.
In time he became a
CHAMPION stopper!

When asked what he'd learned
at the end of the year,
he stopped very still...

The kids started to **CHEER**!

"When I stop and I listen, I can learn to do more!"
Then smiling, he winked, and he dashed out the door.

"Be still and know that I am God."

Psalm 46:10

Made in the USA
Charleston, SC
22 September 2013